John Smith is NOT BORING!

SPACEMAN John THE (NEARLY) BOLD

by Johnny Smith

SCHOLASTIC

To Lottie-Lou, Daisy-Doo ... and Florence too!

Chapter One

"Wow! That is AMAZING!"

I'm lying on the grass in the back garden looking up at the stars. Thousands and thousands of twinkling tiny specks are dotted in the dark night sky.

As a famous scientist once said, space is massive and totally interesting. We studied it in school and we learnt all about stars and shooting stars and something called

asteroids − which was what I thought Granddad had said he had up his bottom.

"How many stars are in the sky, Granddad?"

"Billions," says Granddad, lying next to me on the grass, squinting up at the heavens. "In the great scheme of things, it makes you realize how unimportant you really are."

"He means you," says my big sister, Hayley, working her way down the garden path, folding her girly rags into a washing basket. "How unimportant YOU really are."

Granddad looks at me and smiles. "She doesn't mean it."

"Yes, I do, John Smith," chimes Hayley. "You're the boy with the most boring name in the town, in the country, in the world, in the universe!"

Hayley hums her way into the house, pleased with her addition to the conversation. She's always teasing me over my name.

A ball of fur comes bounding up the garden path. Muffin lives next door with the Virgos. Adam Virgo is a world-champion school bully. He's always happy making my life a misery. And while the entire Virgo family is on holiday in the Costa Del Somewhere-or-other, Muffin, the annoying little flappy-eared cocker spaniel, is living with us,

which is like rolling out the red carpet for the devil.

"What is it, boy?" says Granddad. "What have you found?"

Muffin drops a football at my feet. The air gently hisses out of the bite marks where his fangs have sunk into the leather.

"That's my football!" I moan.

"Oh dear, I think he's punctured it," says Granddad.

Muffin rolls on his back, expecting me to give his tummy a good tickle. He really is the most annoying dog of all time! And now he's burst my ball.

"He needs his squeaky toy," says Granddad, picking up a plastic bunny with a bell round its neck. "Here you go, boy, fetch..."

Granddad throws the squeaky toy down the garden path. Muffin bounces off into the undergrowth. Granddad settles back into position, gazing up at the stars.

"Did you know the light from those stars is millions of years old?"

"About the same age as you, Granddad," I chuckle.

"Cheeky," smiles Granddad.

I love our little chats in the garden, me and Granddad. We talk about EVERYTHING, but our favourite topic is the John Smith Club, which I've just joined.

In the John Smith Club, I get to go on these incredible journeys to faraway places and enjoy amazing adventures. It's a bit of a miracle really, but every John Smith has this massive secret. Just because we've got a boring name doesn't mean we have a boring life!

Granddad's in the club too because he's called John Smith as well, although I always thought he was called Granddad. But Dad's not in the John Smith Club because he's called Steve, and as far as I know, they don't have a Steve Smith club, because that would be too silly.

"Life isn't so bad, Granddad..." I sigh.

"Life is great," says Granddad. "It doesn't get better than this: lying under the stars with my grandson, about to go and watch United in the big match..."

"DISASTER! DISASTER! DISASTER!"

Dad comes running into the garden.

"It's awful ... it's terrible..." wails Dad.

He kicks a watering can down the garden path. Muffin yelps and scuttles into the house with his little squeaky toy in his teeth.

"What's happened?" grunts Granddad, struggling to his feet.

"I can hardly bring myself to say it," scowls Dad.

Granddad looks at me, really worried. Dad's gone as white as a ghost in a snowstorm with a sheet over his head. This must be really bad news. Something horrible must have happened.

"Have a seat, son," says Granddad.

Dad collapses in a deckchair and looks at us, his lips trembling, his eyes watering.

"What is it, Dad?" I gulp. "It can't be as bad as all that, can it?"

"It's worse … MUCH WORSE," he groans.

Hayley sticks her head out of the back door, a wicked smirk written all over her face.

"The television's busted," laughs Hayley.

Dad nods glumly. "I told you it was bad."

"No, no … not today!" I scream. "Not with United in the final! What's wrong with the television? Tell me … tell me … TELL ME!"

"The satellite's gone down," says Hayley, plainly. "Sorry."

"The satellite's gone down?" I mumble, shaking my head. "That's terrible … that's awful … that's…" I suddenly look up at them all. "What's a satellite?"

"It's a big mirror in space," says Granddad. "You need it to beam television pictures around the world."

We all look up to space, hoping to see the broken satellite limping through the sky.

"No satellite, no television," sighs Dad.

"No television, no big match," sighs Granddad.

Nooo!

"No big match, no happy John," says Hayley in an annoying baby voice.

That is literally the worst news in the history of news. Our team is playing in the cup final and we'll be staring at a blank screen.

"You mean there's no television at all?" I mumble.

"That's not quite true," sneers Hayley. "It's not as bad as that."

We all stare hopefully at Hayley.

"I can still watch *The Girly Show* on the Girly Channel because that's on a different satellite," she chuckles.

"Even worse," moans Dad.

"The biggest match in years," protests Granddad, "and we're going to miss it."

"How long until kick-off?" I beg.

"Thirty minutes," he mutters.

I spring to my feet. "Someone needs to

fix the satellite!"

"No kidding?" chuckles Hayley. "What are you going to do, you snivelling little wimp? Climb into your special rocket and take your toolbox twenty thousand miles into deepest, darkest space?"

Wouldn't it be incredible to take a trip into outer space? I could slide down the rings of Saturn, catch the tail of a comet or toast marshmallows on the surface of the sun. And maybe I could fix that dodgy satellite too. Isn't that what the John Smith Club is all about, journeying to faraway places and having great adventures? Well, it doesn't get more far away than outer space!

But this time I've got a real mission! This time I can help my fellow Earth-dwellers, and who knows, maybe they'll even put up a statue of me and write my name on a wall – but this time in a nice way.

I race up the garden path and through the back door.

"Follow me, Granddad!"

I'm going to boldly go where no eight-year-old snivelling wimp has gone before!

Chapter Two

"I can fix the satellite!"

I dash into Granddad's bedroom, dive under the bed and drag out the old chest.

"How are you gonna do that, son?" says Granddad, hobbling into the room behind me.

"I've been a knight, a pirate ... how about a spaceman?" I poke my head round from the side of the bed and fix Granddad with a mischievous look. "And whilst I'm up there, maybe I can find out if the moon really is made of cheese! Imagine, the first ever intergalactic cheese toastie."

"You're trying to change what happens right here on Earth," says Granddad, "using the John Smith Club to go fiddling around with the broken satellite so we can all watch the football on the telly. Nothing like that has ever been done by the John Smith Club before – we keep our adventures separate to the rest of the world. Maybe it won't work!"

"And maybe it will," I reply. "Who's to say us John Smiths can't change the world around us?"

I throw the lid open and stare at the contents.

"Just feast your eyes on this lot," I gasp.

Inside the chest are loads of different costumes – knight helmets, gladiator swords,

pirate hats, spy disguises, cowboy boots ...
and tucked away in the corner, a silver
spacesuit.

"Do you know anything about space,
Granddad?" I murmur.

I jump on the bed and lower my legs
into the spacesuit.

"I just know this one thing about space,"
says Granddad, suddenly really serious. "In
space, no one can hear you scream."

Now that is a horribly scary thought.

"Maybe I should come with you," he nods.

"I fly alone!" I announce dramatically.
"Anyway, I need you to be back here in
mission control. How long have we got until
kick-off?"

Granddad checks his watch. "Twenty-six
minutes and fourteen seconds..." He frowns.
"Thirteen seconds ... twelve seconds ...
eleven seconds..."

I pick up my helmet and put it under my arm. "How do I look, Granddad?"

"Cosmic," beams Granddad. "Every inch the spaceman."

I take a deep breath and say the magic words that will send me on my special quest.

"Say it long, say it loud, I'm John Smith and I'm—"

"Wait, wait, wait," interrupts Granddad.

"What is it?"

"You'll need one of these." Granddad pulls a tiny screwdriver out of his pocket. "This little baby has been with me through thick and thin," he says. "Might be just the thing to mend a wonky satellite."

I take the screwdriver and slip it in my spacesuit pocket.

"OK, this is it, Granddad," I continue. "Oooh, ooh ... wait a moment..."

I've heard that space is a really big place

and, just like Mum and Dad let me play games on really long journeys, I might need some entertainment. So I dash back to my room and grab my mini games console.

"OK, Granddad, this really is it. . ."

I repeat the special words that will launch me on my faraway quest. *"Say it long, say it loud, I'm John Smith and I'm—"*

"WAIT!"

Granddad looks at me sternly. "Do you need the bathroom? Because once you're in space, there's no taking that suit off."

"No, Granddad," I reply. "I do not need the — ooh, you've gone and said it now. I suddenly need a pee. . ."

"Hurry," says Granddad.

I skip to the loo, do my business and skip back again.

"OK," says Granddad, "this really is it. Wait a moment, one final thing. . ."

Granddad looks at me and winks. "Be careful."

"We're running out of time, Granddad. I just want to say the special magic words. *'Say it long, say it loud, I'm John Smith and I'm proud'* and I'll be on my—"

Suddenly I can hear the deafening roar of mighty engines.

"Everyman One, you are cleared for take-off," says Granddad. Then, just like in the space movies I've seen on the telly, Granddad starts the countdown. "Ten … nine … eight … seven…"

"Wish me luck, Granddad!" I cry.

"Six … five … four…"

Everywhere is lit up in flashes of orange and purple and red.

"Three … two … one…"

I'm in the middle of a swirl of smoke and steam. Everything starts shaking.

"LIFT-OFF!"

I'm zooming towards the stars at a gazillion miles an hour. My little home quickly becomes a tiny speck far below.

This is it. Next stop outer space.

"It's one small step for man," I announce, "one giant leap for John Smith..."

Chapter Three

The lights on the flight control panel are sparkling, the monitors are purring, and the two giant furry dice above the flight control panel are bobbing up and down. I'm sitting in the pilot's seat of my spaceship with my hands on the leather steering wheel, hurtling into space faster than a speeding bullet.

I lean forward, snap the glove box open and grab a travel sweet. Butterscotch and caramel, now that is what I call out of this

world!

Suddenly the speaker on the dash crackles into life.

"Come in, Spaceman John. Come in, Spaceman John. This is mission control. Can you hear me?"

"This is Spaceman John, I hear you loud and clear," I reply in my best spaceman's voice.

"Can you repeat that?" says mission control. "I'm not wearing my hearing aid!"

"I said I can hear you, Granddad!" I shout.

"All right," says mission control, "there's no need to shout! Now listen very carefully. I want you to take the spaceship into turbo-thrust-thingy..."

"Turbo-thrust-thingy?" I nod. "How do I do that?"

"It's very simple," says mission control. "Push the big thing marked turbo-thrust-thingy all the way forward. It's that silver stick right in front of you."

Who am I to argue with mission control? I push the silver stick forward. Suddenly the booster rockets power up and the ship zooms even faster into space.

"Waaaa-heeeeyyyyy!!!"

"You are on course for the satellite," says mission control. "Remember, the whole town depends on you. Good luck."

"Thanks, Granddad – I mean, mission control – over and out..."

With my successful spaceship launch behind me, it's time to sit back and enjoy the ride.

So this is space, eh?

I look out of the window and see this incredible planet I've never seen before. It's green and blue with little wisps of cloud floating all around it. Wow! This must be

a brand new planet because it's definitely not like Mars or Jupiter or Saturn, or any of the other planets I've studied in school. This planet looks sort of friendly and nice. I'd like to live on a planet like this green-and-blue blob.

I lift the armrest, root through the music collection and whack on something called "Rocket Man" – just the right kind of music.

"Come in, Spaceman John," says mission control.

"Spaceman John here," I reply. "How can I help you, mission control?"

"You are about to leave the Earth's atmosphere and experience zero gravity, which means you will be completely weightless. It is important you stay buckled in your seat at all times. Do not go spinning round inside the spaceship doing backflips and cartwheels like we've seen spacemen do, treating this as just one big ride in a fairground. Do you copy, Spaceman John? This is an important mission, not a joyride through the stars."

"Waaaa–heeeeyyy . . . this is brilliant!" I shout.

"What are you doing, Spaceman John?" says mission control.

"I'm bouncing round inside the spaceship! I can fly. . ."

"Spaceman John, what did I just say about staying in your seat?"

This is one hundred per cent mega. Everything is floating around with me. The travel sweets are floating out of the tin, the CDs are floating out of the armrest, even the furry dice are floating up to touch the roof of the spaceship.

Zero gravity rocks!

I do a forward roll, bounce off the side of the spaceship, open my mouth and gobble a travel sweet in mid-air. This is right up there with the top three things ANYONE has ever done ANYWHERE in the history of EVERYTHING!

"This is fantastic, Granddad! I mean, mission control."

"Stay focused, Spaceman John," says mission control. "You are in deepest space. What can you see?"

Out of the window I see a massive shiny thing with a big mirror stuck on its side and a bright pink beam bouncing off it.

"Mission control, I think I see the satellite!" I gasp.

"What colour is it, Spaceman John?" says mission control.

"It's, uh, well . . . it's a big pink satellite and, oh − I think I can see pictures of flowers all over it!"

"A big pink satellite with flowers on it?" says mission control.

"And it's got this bright pink light bouncing off the mirror. . ."

"Can you see inside the bright pink light?"

says mission control.

I steer my spaceship as close to the bright pink light as I dare.

"Granddad!"

"Please, call me mission control," says Granddad.

"I can see lots of things in the bright pink light. I can see some people baking a cake ... and a lady in an old-fashioned dress crying into a handkerchief..."

"Stay away from this satellite!" demands mission control. "This is the Girly Satellite beaming back all the girly television shows to Earth, like baking programmes and costume dramas. Do you copy, Everyman One? You must not touch this satellite!"

"Copy that, mission control, I hear you," I reply.

I steer the spaceship past the Girly Satellite and further into space, past the moons of

Jupiter, the rings of Saturn, the Great Bear and his little brother, the Teddy Bear. I see all the things we learnt about in class, including black holes, red dwarfs and blue moons.

I settle back in my seat, flick a slow-motion travel sweet into the air and gobble it up.

"I could get used to this life," I sigh.

I slide my portable games console out of my pocket and start playing space invaders. Pretend space is so much better than real space – there's loads more aliens to kill for a start.

"Take that, you intergalactic demons of death!" I holler. "I'll zap you with my ray gun!"

"Come in, Spaceman John," says mission control. "What's happening up there? It sounds like you're being attacked!"

"Sorry, Granddad, I was just playing my games console," I mumble.

Suddenly the lights on the flight control panel begin to flash and blink. I buckle up and grip the steering wheel.

"Spaceman John, you are approaching the target," says mission control. "What can you see?"

"I see a blue satellite," I reply, "with pictures of racing cars and steam trains and football players!"

"Excellent," says mission control, "that'll be the satellite we're looking for. See if you can get close up."

"OK, mission control," I reply.

I steer the spaceship as close to the satellite as I dare, then I reach down and pull the handbrake on. The spaceship judders to a sudden stop.

"What do I do now, mission control?"

"Find out why the satellite is broken," replies mission control. "Can you see the on/off light on top of the satellite?"

"It's off," I reply.

"Hmmm," says mission control. "I think I know what's happened. The batteries have run out of power."

"What shall I do?"

"You need to put some fresh batteries into the satellite to get it working again. You should find a pack in the armrest between the seats."

I look in the armrest, but except for a packet of chewing gum and some toffee wrappers, it's totally empty.

"There's nothing there, Granddad..."

"Oh dear," says mission control. "What are we going to do?"

My games console!

I turn it over and flip open the battery compartment.

"I have batteries!" I announce triumphantly.

"Good work, Spaceman John," says mission control. "We have seventeen minutes until kick-off. It's time to go to work."

"Roger that," I reply.

"Who's Roger?" says mission control.

"No one," I reply, "that's just what they say."

"All right," says mission control. "Open the hatch and fix the satellite. The future of the football-viewing world depends on it."

Chapter Four

I do exactly what Granddad – I mean mission control – tells me. I screw my helmet on tight, pull on my space gloves and connect my backpack to the oxygen tank. Then I press my palm against the sensor at the side of the space hatch. The space hatch slides open with a *whoosh* and I see the endless stretch of black, starry space in front of me.

"Wow! Space is spacey!" I gasp.

"Spaceman John," says mission control, "we're running out of time."

I float to the satellite and grab hold of one of the big sails. Then I pull myself down the side of the satellite and past the big shiny mirror used to bounce television programmes around the Earth.

"Come on, come on," says mission control, "we only have fourteen minutes until the start of the match..."

I catch my reflection in the mirror and see my little head inside my space helmet. I give myself a wink. I think I'm going to remember this moment for a very long time.

"The battery compartment, Spaceman John..." says mission control.

I see a little plastic flap on the underside of the satellite.

"I've found the battery compartment, mission control."

"Excellent," says mission control. "Flip out
the old batteries and replace them with the
new ones. And be quick about it – I'm
busting for a pee!"

"I'm on it, Granddad. Sorry – mission
control."

I take out the screwdriver, open the battery compartment, pluck the dead batteries out and drop them into space.

Then I slot three fresh batteries in the satellite, making sure I've got them the right way around.

"Hurry!" says mission control.

I clip the last battery into the compartment.

"I've done it, mission control!" I cheer.

Suddenly I hear a deep throbbing inside the satellite. The on/off light pings into life and lots of little lights chase one another up and down the two giant sails at the side of the satellite. Finally, the giant mirror glows a deep blue.

"You've done it, Spaceman John," announces mission control.

A light strikes the mirror and bounces off into space.

"I can see the television beam!" I gasp.

"Can you see inside it?" says mission control.

"I can see people arriving at a football stadium ... and three men in suits in a television studio..."

"Well done, John," chuckles mission control, "you've fixed the satellite."

"What do I do now, Granddad?"

"Come home, Spaceman John," says mission control. "You've got twelve minutes until the match starts. Plenty of time to get your spaceship back to Earth and settle in for some top-flight footy. In the meantime, I'm off to pay a visit to the little boy's room..."

"Roger that, mission control, over and out!"

I push myself off the satellite and float gently back to the spaceship.

Mission accomplished.

Chapter Five

I settle into my seat, buckle my belt, power up my spaceship and head for home. Goodbye, little satellite. Goodbye, space. I'm going to watch United win the final.

The rockets roar as I turn the spaceship in a big circle and steer her towards Earth.

I might be on the far side of the Milky Way but an empty tummy is an empty tummy. Time I found myself a little space snack.

I ping the glove box open and search around for another travel sweet. "Oh dear. . ."

The box is completely empty.

I unbuckle my belt and float off looking for a nibble. As I drift to the back of the spaceship, I see a big cupboard.

Space Food, reads the sign on the door. "What have we got in here?"

I've heard all about space food – bite-sized morsels that taste like entire meals. Burger and chips! Sticky toffee pudding! Cheese toasties! The mind boggles!

Inside the cupboard are lots of little cardboard cartons in neat rows. I pull a carton off the shelf.

"Chicken chow mein. . ."

I flip the special space carton over and read off the back.

"Oodles of noodles in a finger-licking chicken sauce."

Scrum-diddly-umptious!

"Heat in special space cooker for six minutes. Check product is piping hot before serving."

I whack the space food in the space cooker until it makes a little ding. It tastes just like the ready meals Mum brings home from the supermarket. I close my eyes and savour the delicious tastes.

"Mmmmmmmm..."

When I open my eyes, I am face-to-face with another spaceman, staring right back at me!

The spaceman lunges at me, making a horrible growl. Underneath his helmet I see big bulging eyes and a nasty, drooling mouth.

"AAAAARRRRGGGHHHH!!!"

I push away and go spinning head over heels, crashing into the flight control panel, accidentally nudging the turbo-thrust-thingy with my bottom.

The boosters flare up; the rockets spit fire into space. The spaceship kicks on at a million miles a second. The lights start flashing on the flight control panel, the alarm starts beeping. The furry dice are flying about like crazy.

"Mission control, mission control, do you read me?" I scream. Then I remember, mission control is sitting on the loo reading a copy of the *Racing Times*.

Suddenly the darkness of space is lit up with flashes of bright white light. Out of the window I see we're heading for a comet!!!

I dive for the steering wheel and turn the spaceship sideways. As I do, the spaceman does a somersault and crashes into me.

"Get off me! Get off me!" I gasp.

We strike the tail of the comet.

The spaceship goes spinning round in circles. Lumps of comet smash into the side of the spaceship; fire scorches the nose. Ice

peppers the windscreen. I try pressing the windscreen wipers but they jam. Outside, red-hot flames lick at the window.

"Mission control, mission control, do you copy?" I holler, desperately.

The radio crackles into life.

"Everyman One, this is mission control, sorry about that. I just nipped off for a rich tea biscuit and I thought whilst I was in that part of the world I might like to make myself a nice cup of tea..."

"Mission control, we have a problem!"

"So anyway, I made myself a cup of tea, and do you know what? I couldn't find the sugar..."

"Mission control, we have a problem!" I repeat.

"So I had to borrow a spoon of sugar from whatshername next door..." says mission control. "You know, her with the leg..."

"MISSION CONTROL!!!"

"Anyway, how can I be of service?"

"There's another spaceman in the spaceship!" I scream.

"Don't be daft, Spaceman John," says mission control. "This is a one-man flight."

"Oh no!" I shriek.

The spaceship is hurtling towards a massive, lifeless rock.

"I think we're going to crash, Granddad," I cry.

"You're breaking up on me," says mission control. "Say that again..."

"Crash positions!"

The spaceship slams into the rock.

The hatch explodes and we both fall out at a zillion miles an hour. We tumble across the craters, wrapped up in each other's arms and legs, one big spacemen bundle, with the spaceship skidding just behind us.

Eventually we roll to a stop.

I scramble to my feet and holler at the other spaceman.

"You made me crash my spaceship..."

The spaceman takes a step towards me. This is the most scared I've been since I slept head to toe with Hayley in the same bed.

I peer into the helmet and see the face on the inside in all its amazing detail. It is a face that turns my heart ice cold with fear.

Chapter Six

"Muffin!"

It's the annoying little spaniel from next door, inside his very own spacesuit, with his squeaky bunny in his teeth. The dog we're meant to be keeping safe and well while the Virgo family holiday in the Costa Del Somewhere-or-other. Instead, he's stolen a ride to the far side of the universe.

"Muffin! What are you doing here?"

Muffin looks at me and cocks an ear. Then he sticks his big pink tongue out and licks the inside of the space visor. I pull his helmet off and stare at him.

"Bad dog! You crashed my spaceship!"

Muffin barks and runs round in a little circle, his tail sticking out of the back of his spacesuit. How did he end up on the mission with me? He must have sneaked off and snuffled his way into the chest under Granddad's bed. So when I said the magic words he got taken on the journey by accident.

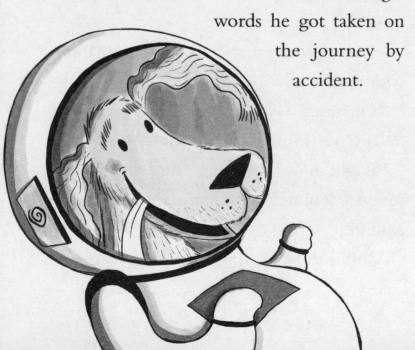

Granddad comes crackling through the radio in my helmet.

"Come in, Everyman One... Come in, Everyman One..."

"This is Everyman One, do you copy?" I reply.

"Are you all right?" says mission control.

"I've crashed my spaceship," I gulp. "And I'm not alone..."

"Not alone?" says mission control. "You mean you have encountered an alien life form?"

"You could say that," I nod. "I have Muffin with me!"

"Oh dear," says mission control. "I hope he behaves himself. What's he doing?"

"Right now," I grunt, "he's chasing his squeaky toy over the intergalactic landscape. Muffin!"

Muffin stops chasing his squeaky toy and

54

looks at me, his flappy ears floating above his head.

"Perhaps if he hears my voice, he'll be a good doggy," says Granddad. "Mission control to Muffin! Mission control to Muffin! Can you hear me, Muffin? What's he doing now?"

"He's running round in little circles chasing his tail," I reply.

"Where are you, Spaceman John?" says Mission Control.

"I'm on some faraway planet, mission control," I reply. "It's very cold and very dark."

"How is the spaceship? Is it damaged?"

Just then the spaceship groans and splutters, the lights fizzle out and the engine wheezes and croaks to a stop.

"We're in trouble, mission control," I sigh. "You'll have to watch the football match without me."

"Can you get help?" says mission control.

"Help! Where am I going to get help?" I protest. "Oh, Granddad, why did I ever come on this mission? Wait a moment, I'm being a real space cadet! I can say the magic words and beam myself right back into the living room in time for the match!"

I bundle Muffin into my arms, take a big breath and speak the words...

"Say it long, say it loud – I'm John Smith and I'm PROUD!"

But nothing happens. I stay rooted to the spot, a long way from home.

"What's happening, Granddad? It's not working!"

"Yes," mumbles Granddad. "I remember now, I had the same problem when I went to Pluto once. The magic doesn't work in space."

"WHAT!!!"

"I know, you can imagine my surprise. I had to hitch a ride home on a shooting star. Very inconvenient."

"What am I going to do, Granddad?"

"You're going to have to get back the same way you got there – in that spaceship!"

Suddenly I see something incredible. A little ball comes bouncing over the brow of a hill and trickles down a small path, rolling to a stop at my feet.

"It's a golf ball," I blurt.

Just then, the ground starts to rumble. Muffin scrambles over the alien landscape, slipping and sliding on the icy slope, and hides behind a rock.

"What's going on?" says mission control.

Coming over the brow of the hill is a funny-looking silver car. As it gets nearer I see it is actually hovering off the ground. It glides down through the rocks and pauses a few feet away from us. On the back of the car is a set of golf clubs.

The entire roof of the car softly rises up and a little blue head in a golf visor pokes out from the side, surrounded by swirling wisps of steam.

"Aha!" says the little blue head.

He points a long thin finger at the golf ball and magically lifts it into the air.

"Fancy a lift?" says the little blue head. "Hop in!"

Chapter Seven

The little blue head is attached to a long blue body. The funny little blue man sits in the driver's seat, carefully steering his little car over the icy wasteland. I sit with Muffin huddled up on the back seat of the car, staring out of the window.

"Welcome to our frozen planet," says the little blue man. His head spins completely round and he smiles at us. "We don't get many vistors round these parts – not any more.

He looks into the sky at a dark planet over our heads.

"We used to be a regular tourist stop," continues the little blue man, "but if you can't guarantee the sunshine, you can't get the tourists. We tried some winter sports – bit of skiing, some ice skating – but it never really caught on.

I sit quietly on the back seat of the car, letting the little blue man ramble on.

"My name is Quantum, by the way," he says cheerily.

Quantum steers his little car over the mountains and down into a giant crater. The doors ping open and we step outside.

"You should meet our leader," says Quantum. "He would find you most interesting. Did I tell you we haven't had a visitor for a very long time?"

"Uh, once or twice," I reply, slipping after Quantum over the ice. "Come on, Muffin..."

Quantum leads us to a huge tower made of ice. We step inside, the doors close and with a *whoosh* we are carried to the very top of the tower.

I see loads of aliens standing in the twinkling light, all shapes and sizes and colours – three eyes, two eyes or twelve eyes, sometimes with four heads, sometimes without any heads at all. But even though they all look different, they have one thing in common. They all wear really thick woolly jumpers. Muffin clings nervously to my shins as we walk by.

Suddenly a little ginger-headed man appears on a slab of ice with a crown on his head.

"This is our alien king," whispers Quantum.

Quantum walks forward and addresses the alien king.

"Your Majesty, we have visitors..."

The alien king looks at me, then trains his curious little eyes on Muffin – all six of them.

"We have known for some time there is intelligent life on your planet," says the alien king.

"Well, I like to think I know what I'm doing," I reply.

"Be quiet, fool!" says the alien king.

A lightning bolt zaps the ground. The ice melts, runs to water, then quickly freezes again.

"I am talking to the leader of your mission," says the alien king.

The alien king steps down from his little slab of ice and walks up to Muffin. Muffin plops his tongue out of his mouth and does two little barks. The alien king nods.

"He says he comes from a planet far away," says the alien king, addressing all the other aliens.

Muffin continues his barking.

"And this is his co-pilot," continues the alien king. "Squeaky!"

Muffin makes Squeaky squeak a few times. The aliens copy him, making little squawking, squeaking sounds themselves.

The alien king raises an arm and everyone

falls silent.

"And who is this buffoon?" demands the alien king.

He turns and looks at me. Before I can open my mouth, Muffin barks a few times more. The alien king turns again to all the other aliens to explain.

"He says this is his earthling servant," says the alien king. "And he goes by the name of John Smith..."

The aliens laugh even harder.

"Your name is very common," says the alien king. "On our planet it is the same name as Zargon Queegleblaster. An extremely common name."

"Actually, on my planet, my name is very rare," I lie.

Muffin barks again.

"Commander Muffin says you lie. He says you have a very boring name. He says it is written in the stars," says the alien king.

"And on the back of the gym wall," I moan defiantly.

"Why have you come to our little planet?" says the alien king. "There is nothing here to see."

"We crashed into your planet by accident," I reply.

"I knew you didn't come deliberately," says the alien king. "Our little planet is sick."

They're always saying things like that in films about distant planets. He's probably going to give us his "our sun is dying" speech next.

"The sun that sits in our sky and gives us light and warmth is dying," sighs the alien king. "Without light or warmth we will soon die too."

The aliens coo in a really sad way – really sad alien cooing.

"Take this fool to the Chamber of Endless

Reflection," says the alien king, pointing at me. "Where he might sit by the Lake of Thought Bubbles and sup the Water of . . ."

The aliens lean in, waiting for the king to finish his sentence.

"The Water of . . . ?" says the king's assistant, Quantum.

"The Water of . . . Splishy Sploshy Wetness," says the alien king. "Do all this whilst I talk further with the leader of the mission – Commander Muffin."

The alien king looks at Muffin, who pants a few times and dangles his slobbery tongue out of his mouth.

"You've got it all wrong," I complain as the aliens drag me away. "I'm the leader of the mission. On Planet Earth, he's just a dog with a squeaky toy!"

Muffin does a really long growl. The alien king looks at Muffin and nods, like he actually understands what Muffin is saying!

"Really? That is most interesting," says the alien king.

"What does he say?" I holler.

"He says we should throw you in a cage and feed you stale biscuits," says the alien king. "Very well, then — take this idiot to the Chamber of Endless Reflection!"

The aliens move in to drag me away again.

I appeal one final time to the alien king. "We can help you!"

"How can you help me?" He laughs.

"Fix our spaceship," I reply, "and maybe we can save your planet."

"Tell me more," says the alien king.

"We can bring you endless sunshine," I announce. "But first, our broken spaceship. . ." The aliens gather round the spaceship, especially the aliens with fifteen arms and two or three brains and brilliant

DIY skills.

"Very well, let us mend your spaceship, earthling," says the alien king.

The aliens set to work, fixing the

rockets, patching up the panels, mending the windows. Finally, I get the chewing gum from inside the spaceship and stick the door back on its hinges. Soon our spaceship is back to its fighting best.

The alien king steps forward.

"Farewell, Commander Muffin," says the alien king. "I hope you and your pet, John Smith, have a safe journey home. Here is something to remember us by. . ."

The alien king puts a fistful of ice in the palm of my hand.

"That's great, thanks," I smile.

You'd think he could have coughed up some moon gold.

Muffin scampers towards the spaceship, then turns and barks a few times.

"He says go in peace, people of wonder," says the alien king.

I walk to the spaceship, pausing by

Quantum to whisper in his ear. "You know and I know, your alien king has been making the whole thing up. This is just a dog. What goes on between his flappy ears, no one knows, especially not your king."

Muffin barks again.

"What did he say?" says the alien king.

"Commander Muffin says he's sorry about his pet," says Quantum.

"Now for your part of the deal, Commander Muffin," says the alien king. "You must save our planet."

"And he *will* save your planet," I reply, "for he has a brilliant plan. Isn't that right, Commander Muffin?"

Commander Muffin plops his tongue out of his mouth and pants.

I must be true to my word, I'm about to do the hardest thing I've ever done in my tiny little life. I am about to wreck my chances

72

of watching United play the biggest match in the club's history. And it won't be just me who'll be missing out. The whole town will either be staring at a blank screen or, worse, watching a programme about ponies or ballet dancers OR BOTH on the Girly Channel.

Completely gutted and sick as a parrot,

I fly the spaceship back to the satellite and move it into a new position. The sun's rays bounce off the mirror and fall on to the alien planet below. I imagine the aliens are dancing and singing, bathed in the glow of the sunshine, chanting Muffin's name.

Meanwhile, Muffin is lying on the floor of the spaceship, gnawing away at his squeaky bunny.

"Mission control, can you hear me?"

"Loud and clear, Spaceman John. Come home. The match starts in five minutes."

"Change of plan, mission control," I reply. "I've had to use the satellite to save a tiny, dying planet. We won't be watching the football match."

I fire up the rockets, buckle myself in my seat and release the handbrake.

"Come on, Muffin," I sigh. "We're going

home."

Halfway across the oceans of space, the rockets flicker and burn out. The spaceship drifts silently, then stops. A light flashes on the flight-control panel with a little symbol of a petrol pump next to it.

"We've run out of fuel, Muffin," I gulp. "What are we going to do?"

Chapter Eight

Muffin's not listening to me. He's got his head wedged in the space-food cupboard.

"Muffin, we're drifting in space and you've got your snout in the food!"

Muffin falls out of the cupboard, an extra-fiery chilli con carne ready meal splodged on the end of his nose.

"Oh, Muffin, what have you gone and done?"

He screws his face up tight and gasps a

red-hot breath. His eyes begin to water. His tongue plops out of his mouth.

I hear a gurgle, then a grumble, then a deep rumbling as the chilli goes to work, lighting a fire in the poor pup's belly.

This is going to be a heck of a bottom explosion!

Wait a minute, he's just given me an idea.

Two minutes later. . .

"Go on, Muffin, you can do it!!!"

Muffin has his bottom squeezed out of the spaceship window and – well, there's no way of putting this nicely – he's doing the greatest fart in the universe. Talk about a cosmic wind!

"Well done, Muffin," I holler.

The spaceship bombs through the solar system, tearing past fiery Mars, ice-cold Venus and mysterious Mercury.

"Keep it up, boy," I cheer.

You know, I hate to admit it, but after the adventure we've had today, and seeing how the spaceship is actually being powered by Muffin's bottom, I've grown to quite like my little friend.

"You're not such a bad doggy after all," I smile, patting Muffin on the head.

Suddenly I hear a terrible, low gurgling. Muffin scrunches his nose up and narrows his eyes. I think he's about to do the mother of all intergalactic botty burps!

The spaceship goes spinning off course, tumbling and toppling through space.

"Oh no!" I shriek.

I throw myself in the pilot's seat and grab the leather steering wheel.

"Hold tight, Muffin. . ."

Muffin pulls his ears over his eyes and dives under the seat.

I wrestle the controls, twisting the spaceship this way and that, pushing the turbo-thrust-thingy, slamming on the brakes.

I see a large shiny pink object in the top corner of the windscreen hurtling towards us. It's the Girly Satellite ... and we're heading straight for it!

"Crash positions, Muffin..."

SMASH!

"I think we've just totalled the Girly Satellite," I chuckle.

Lots of pink petals float past the window. The spaceship stops spinning and settles itself again. I square myself in the pilot's seat and take a deep breath. Muffin pokes his head out and pulls his ears away from his eyes.

"Everything is under control, Muffin," I smile.

When I look out of the window again, I see the mysterious green-and-blue planet with wispy clouds I saw earlier. Muffin sees it too and starts barking. Then I understand. The mysterious green and blue planet with little wisps of grey cloud is Planet Earth. It looks like a really nice place to be.

"Come on, Muffin," I sigh, "it's time we went home..."

Chapter Nine

As we get closer to Earth, the spaceship starts to jiggle and bounce around. Muffin digs a space in my lap, curled up in a little ball, his tail tucked underneath his bottom. Outside the spaceship, a fire is raging. The windows are glowing white hot.

"Prepare for a crash landing, Muffin," I yell.

We fall out of space and into the clouds. The fire turns to rain and then, suddenly,

the clouds have vanished and I see my house below me.

"Come in, Spaceman John," says mission control on the radio.

"Spaceman John here," I reply.

"Get ready to land..."

I close my eyes and WHUMP, we crash in a heap on Granddad's bed. I struggle to my feet and look around for Muffin. He rolls out from under the sheets with his squeaky toy in his teeth.

"Are you all right, Muffin?" I gasp.

Muffin looks at me and nods, his eyes burning brightly.

"John, John," exclaims Granddad, "you made it back!"

Granddad gives me a great big hug.

"I had to use the satellite to save the alien planet, Granddad," I reply. "We're going to miss the match."

"You did the right thing, John," replies Granddad. He sits next to me on the bed and puts his arm around me. "I'm proud of you."

I look at him and smile.

"Life isn't so bad, Granddad," I grin.

"Life is great," says Granddad. "Trust me, it doesn't get better than this."

And we both burst out laughing.

"DISASTER! DISASTER! DISASTER!"

Hayley comes running into Granddad's bedroom.

"It's awful ... it's terrible..." she wails.

"What is?" I gulp.

"They're not showing my girly television any more," she protests. "They're showing the FOOTBALL instead! They say there's a problem with the satellite and it's only picking up boys' programmes..."

I run downstairs to see for myself.

"Look, Granddad, it's the football!" I cheer.

The spaceship must have crashed into the Girly Satellite and knocked it off course, straight into the boys' satellite television beam.

Granddad settles next to me on the sofa. We kick our shoes off and wait for the referee to blow the whistle for the start of the match. Even Muffin gets in on the action, jumping into my lap with Squeaky in his teeth.

"Well done, John," chuckles Granddad. "You did good work today."

"And well done, Muffin," I smile.

The referee blows his whistle and the match kicks off.

"COME ON, UNITED!"

Have you read

John Smith's other

NOT
BORING!

adventures?

Take a look at another NOT BORING adventure!

John Smith is NOT BORING!

SHERIFF John THE (PARTLY) WILD

by Johnny Smith

A horse whinnies; a shadow moves across the saloon doors.

The doors fly open.

A stranger in a massive Mexican hat stumbles into the saloon. The barman hides behind the bar, the piano player stops playing and everyone looks around nervously. Why is everybody so scared?

The stranger walks slowly between the tables, chewing a piece of gum.

He leans over the bar and pulls out a jug of liquor.

"Did you see what he just did?" I mumble. "Somebody should call the sheriff."

"You are the sheriff!" whispers Little Joe.

"Oh yes, I forgot," I giggle. "Sorry about that."

The stranger looks at me for a really long time and he chews and he chews and he chews. Then he turns and spits into the spittoon.

"So, you're the new sheriff, yeah..." he says.

"Oh yes," I reply, confidently. "Sheriff by name, sheriff by nature."

I have absolutely no idea what I'm talking about.

"That so, huh?" he replies. "And what is your name, sheriff?"

OK, here we go, I'm going to let him have it — both barrels.

"My name is John Smith," I announce.

There is a bit of a pause before the stranger cracks up laughing.

"Seriously, sheriff," he grunts, "what is your name?"

Oh dear, I just gave it my best shot and he fell about in hysterical hoots. I fix him with my meanest stare as I try to think up a new name for myself. I'd better make this good. After all, they've all got exciting names in the Wild West — Butch this and Sundance that.

"What's the matter, sheriff, can't you speak?" he grins.

"I'm thinking!" I reply.

I carry on thinking for a little bit longer. Everyone leans in, waiting for me to answer. Suddenly, my new name hits me in a blinding moment of genius.

"They call me the Sheriff with No Name!" I growl.

Everyone nods. I think they like the sound of this. It is a very mysterious name.

"That's a very mysterious name," says the stranger. "What's your business here, sheriff?"

"I'm here to protect our cattle from El Bandido," I reply.

"Oooh," says the stranger, "El Bandido! I hear many bad things about this El Bandido — that he is a monster, a villain, an outlaw. I heard he even stole the piñata from a children's birthday party and ate all the candy! And I ask myself: can all this be true?"

The stranger looks round the saloon, drumming his fingers on the bar. "Tell me, where are you taking your cattle? Are you taking them to Cactus City?"

"Yes," I reply. "It's my job to make sure

the cattle don't fall into the hands of El Bandido."

"You don't say," laughs the stranger. "What does he look like, this El Bandido?"

"They say he's got pure gold teeth and his breath smells like a rotten, pongy bottom!"

The stranger suddenly flashes a golden grin.

"You mean it smells like this!" he snarls.

He blows a jet of air in my face. Satan's bum-hole, that stinks!

I stare at the stranger, my eyes popping. "You're El Bandido!"

"Of course," he roars. The stranger throws back his hat. "My horse was bitten in the rear by a rattlesnake," he grunts. "So I sucked out the poison! That is why I have, as you say, breath like a rotten, pongy bottom!"

Wow, he must be one tough cookie, this El Bandido. A whole packet of tough cookies!

"Do you know what my name means in your language?" he growls.

"Uh, the bandit?" I reply.

"OK, so you guessed," he sighs. "But I am still as dangerous as a scorpion in a slipper!"

"We're not scared of you, El Bandido, are we, good people of Dungville?" I cry.

The good people of Dungville have their

heads under the tables and their bottoms in the air.

"Dungville," sneers El Bandido. "The only thing this stinky little town is good for is poop, cowpats, jobbies. Do you know the sound the church bell makes? Dung! Dung! Dung!"

El Bandido cackles for a really long time. When he sees no one else is joining in with his silly joke, he shakes his head. "El Bandido is wasted on you lot!" he shrugs.

Suddenly El Bandido rolls a long leather whip out from under his coat and sends it flicking and cracking across the room. "If you were in my gang, I would soon whip you into shape!" he guffaws.

He slams his glass on the table and does a loud burp. "I would like to thank you for the useful tip about the cattle, Sheriff No-Name," he grins. "My compadres will be waiting for you at our secret hideaway up in the hills."

El Bandido cackles to himself, then dashes out of the saloon with great gusto.

"Are you crazy, sheriff?" says Little Joe. "You just told El Bandido our whole plan. Now he'll be waiting for us. He'll steal our cattle and sell them in the market. And we'll be ruined! RUINED!"

Oh no, I've really goofed this time. Everyone in the saloon stares at me, eyes bulging, mouths wide open.

"Tell us you can protect our cattle, sheriff," says Old Jake.

"Don't worry," I reply. "I'll make sure we get the cattle safely to market. After all, I'm the sheriff and what I say goes!"

Other

NOT

BORING!

adventures from

John Smith

John Smith is NOT BORING!
CAP'N John THE (SLIGHTLY) FIERCE
by Johnny Smith

Johnny Smith is an experienced animation and live-action screenwriter. As one half of Sprackling and Smith, the comedy screenwriting team, he sold numerous original feature film scripts here and in Hollywood, including Disney's box office hit GNOMEO & JULIET. He lives in London with his wife and children.